D0210891

MOBY SHINOBI

NINJA ON THE JOB

JACKSON COUNTY LIBRARY, MEDFORD, OR

JUN   2019

by Luke Flowers

SCHOLASTIC INC.

FOR MY MOM AND DAD —
WHO BUILT A STRONG FOUNDATION OF ENCOURAGEMENT THROUGHOUT MY LIFE THAT HELPED ME HONE MY CREATIVE NINJA SKILLS. I AM FOREVER GRATEFUL FOR THE GIFT OF GROWING UP IN A HOME FILLED WITH HEARTY LAUGHTER, WACKY CREATIVITY, AND A BOUNTY OF LOVE.

Copyright © 2019 by Luke Flowers

All rights reserved. Published by Scholastic Inc., *Publishers since 1920.* SCHOLASTIC and associated logos are trademarks and/or registered trademarks of Scholastic Inc.

The publisher does not have any control over and does not assume any responsibility for author or third-party websites or their content.

No part of this publication may be reproduced, stored in a retrieval system, or transmitted in any form or by any means, electronic, mechanical, photocopying, recording, or otherwise, without written permission of the publisher. For information regarding permission, write to Scholastic Inc., Attention: Permissions Department, 557 Broadway, New York, NY 10012.

This book is a work of fiction. Names, characters, places, and incidents are either the product of the author's imagination or are used fictitiously, and any resemblance to actual persons, living or dead, business establishments, events, or locales is entirely coincidental.

Library of Congress Cataloging-in-Publication Data

Names: Flowers, Luke, author, illustrator. | Flowers, Luke. Moby Shinobi.
Title: Ninja on the job / by Luke Flowers.
Description: New York, NY : Scholastic Inc., 2019. | Series: Moby Shinobi |
Summary: Told in rhyme, Moby Shinobi tries to help out the construction workers building a house, but as usual his ninja skills just create chaos—until he saves a puppy that has gotten stuck in wet concrete.
Identifiers: LCCN 2018033243| ISBN 9781338256147 (pbk.) | ISBN 9781338256154 (hardcover)
Subjects: LCSH: Ninja—Juvenile fiction. | Helping behavior—Juvenile fiction. | House construction—Juvenile fiction. | Construction workers—Juvenile fiction. | Stories in rhyme. | CYAC: Stories in rhyme. | Ninja—Fiction. Helpfulness—Fiction. | House construction—Fiction. | Construction workers—Fiction. | LCGFT: Stories in rhyme. | Humorous fiction. Classification: LCC PZ8.3.F672 Nk 2019 | DDC [E]—dc23 LC record available at https://lccn.loc.gov/2018033243

10 9 8 7 6 5 4 3 2 1   19 20 21 22 23

Printed in the U.S.A.   88
First printing 2019
Book design by Steve Ponzo

Throw! Dash! Chop! I WOW all my friends.

Grab! Spin! Whoosh! The fun never ends.

Zoom! Swing! Ha! This is such a thrill!

6

8

Moby thinks of a ninja chop!
He puts a piece of wood on top.

CHOP!

CRACK!

AHHH! These broken boards will NOT do!
Let's find a different job for you.

13

Moby thinks of a fast attack.
He prepares for a double whack!

SPIN!

SMACK!

SNAP!

SMASH!

Moby thinks of his ninja cart.
He knows just where he needs to start!

PUSH!

DUMP!

WHOOSH!

BOOM!

25

27

**Moby thinks of a giant climb.
He knows he does not have much time!**